SPEAKER OF TREACHERY

CONNOR WHITELEY

No part of this book may be reproduced in any form or by any electronic or mechanical means. Including information storage, and retrieval systems, without written permission from the author except for the use of brief quotations in a book review.

This book is NOT legal, professional, medical, financial or any type of official advice.

Any questions about the book, rights licensing, or to contact the author, please email connorwhiteley@connorwhiteley.net

Copyright © 2024 CONNOR WHITELEY

All rights reserved.

DEDICATION
Thank you to all my readers without you I couldn't do what I love.

CHAPTER 1

Sebastian Crawley sat on an icy cold metal bench (that was actually his excuse of a bed) inside his little barred prison cell. The cell itself wasn't quite as bad as he had heard from the various elements of the criminal underworld that he had heard of over the years, but it certainly wasn't a five-star luxury hotel.

The cell was disgustingly small with it being two metres by two metres in all directions, with thick steel metal bars forming three walls of his little cage, and a solid steel wall (that Sebastian firmly believed was in front of an escape hatch if only he could cut it open) formed the back wall.

The entire cell stunk of pee, poo and other foulness that Sebastian didn't even want to think about. There wasn't a mattress, pillow or anything that Sebastian had always taken for granted when he had been a Commander of the Empire Army. It never mattered what battlefield he was in, he always had the best equipment and luxurious items that the men under his command could only dream about.

And they always dreamed about his coffee supply in particular.

The foul sound of people shouting, cursing and pounding their fists against their metal bars made Sebastian look outside through the immense metal bars and out onto the corridor his cell was on.

He had no idea what part of the blade-like prison ship he was on, he could have been near the bow, rear or midsections of the ship. There was also no way to tell it from the humming and minor vibrations of the engines.

That was exactly how Sebastian normally told what part of the ship he was in, but he couldn't. These damn prison ships were far too well built for that and the extremely long line of prison cells probably stretched on for a good kilometre or two, and Sebastian really hated to imagine how many prisoners were on this floor alone. Maybe two thousand or ten thousand.

And it wasn't exactly like the corridor was anything to write home about because it had an ugly black metal floor and metal ceiling and its walls were lined with prison cells. There weren't any Prison Guard Drones, protection officers or anything.

If there was a medical emergency, a riot or anything then Sebastian hated to imagine what would happen. But he wasn't completely ignorant to what happened to the criminals of The Great Human Empire. As soon as someone was believed to commit a crime, especially one as horrific as treachery against the Emperor (like anyone on this level was meant to have done), they lost all rights and weren't worth anything more than an insect.

There were so many prisoners that it was just so confusing as to why Sebastian was here in the first place.

He had been fighting, serving and protecting the amazing Empire on some foul jungle world when the Military Police Units of the Empire Army arrested him for treachery and put him personally onto this prison ship. Of course because he was now a criminal in the eyes of the Empire he loved, he had no rights. He couldn't even ask what his actual crime was.

Sebastian was innocent.

"Make sure this prisoner is kept alive at all costs," a slightly high-pitched man said.

Sebastian didn't bother going up to the icy cold bars of his prison cell like the hundreds of other prisoners, because he could see a few cells up there was a man with a black-uniformed prison guard focusing on a prisoner.

Sebastian had to admit the high-pitched man was hot as hell. He was extremely fit, skinny and in his full-on blue battle armour with a logo of the ever-watchful eye of the Inquisition on his chest plate, Sebastian felt his heart skip a few beats. The man couldn't have been more beautiful and even as the man looked around and Sebastian saw his bright red eyes, he actually didn't care.

The man was simply beautiful.

"My Master wants this prisoner no matter what," the man said to the guard. "No accidents but I am not blind to the works of the Prisoner Core. Feel free to kill and torture any of the mutants and traitorous scum on this ship,"

"Of course my Lord," the guard said.

Sebastian turned his attention away from the hot man (as hard as that was considering he probably wasn't going to see another hot man for centuries) and focused on the disgusting prisoner in the cell the hot man was interested in.

The traitor herself wasn't too remarkable because she had been stripped of her clothes, her cybernetic earing attachments had been ripped out making two gaping holes in the side of her head but the woman was still grinning, like she knew something no one else did.

Sebastian really wished he was still an Empire Army Commander with his gun so he could feel a little safer but he didn't have anything. He had only his wit, strength and belief in the Emperor, for all that was worth now the Empire believed him to be a traitor.

"Like this one," the hot man said standing in front of Sebastian's cells. "Do whatever you wish with this one,"

Sebastian weakly smiled at the hot man.

"Tell me traitor how do you want to die?" the hot man asked.

Sebastian shook his head. "I am loyal to the throne. I am loyal to the Emperor. I am guilty of no crime,"

The hot man laughed. "Everyone says that and everyone is guilty on this floor of treachery against the Emperor. There is no greater crime against humanity so rest assured traitor that you will die by the blade of righteousness and you will never be able to atone for your sins against the Emperor,"

Sebastian didn't dare laugh or anything because he partly wanted to make the hot man believe that he was innocent. If anyone could help him escape this prison ship it was him. Even the agents of the Inquisition had immense power over the Empire.

Maybe Sebastian could get this hottie to help him.

But the hot man simply walked away and someone started tapping the cold metal bars of their cell to get his attention.

Sebastian looked over to the traitor the hot man had been interested in and she smiled.

"Don't worry little human," she said. "Your death will come a lot sooner than that when my friends show up,"

CHAPTER 2

As much as Inquisitorial Agent Leo Dawson loved his Master, Inquisitor Mason, he had to admit that he just wasn't a fan of prison ship duty. He normally loved hunting down traitors, torturing them and helping the Empire to become a safer place for everyone no matter if they were a man, woman or child.

He wasn't some traitor babysitter. Leo's skills was in combat, data analysing and basically doing anything that wasn't prisoner escort duty.

Even the damn prison guards were starting to creep him out as Leo walked down the immense prison cell corridor. The sheer echo of is footsteps off the metal floor and ceiling was a little off-putting, and the prisoners were just disgusting.

At least all the immense steel cell bars seemed to be perfectly intact, so Leo simply placed his hands on both his pistols just to be on the safe side. If any of the prison bars did break and the prisoners escaped then he was going to kill them.

No matter what his Master's orders were.

Leo was just glad that even though his Master was currently hunting down traitors and alien forces on a major Hive world five solar systems away, he had been kind enough to lend Leo his fully cloaked warship.

So at least if anything went wrong the warship was close to lend a helping hand. But as far as Leo was concerned this was just a ship filled with criminals and criminals were hardly smart enough to be a threat to an Inquisitorial Agent.

He hoped.

He had always known that the traitors were foul, disgusting people that were deranged for turning their backs on the Emperor, but to see them just sitting here was unreal. Like there was one traitor in a cell to his left that had massive puffy eyes, no mouth and missing ears. Leo had no idea why the man would ever allow the traitors to do that to him.

They all deserved to die no matter what they looked like and no matter how little their crimes were.

Of course when it came to betraying the Emperor, no crime whatsoever was too little to earn the death sentence but clearly some people in the Empire's Government didn't agree, because most of these people were heading to labour camps.

Leo wasn't exactly sure if he liked the idea of labour camps. They would be sent to some mining world, fitted with explosive collars so if they escaped or rioted their heads would explode (that was good) but traitors had to die. That was the way of the Empire, Inquisition and every one of sound mind.

Leo passed another man with no teeth, no eyes and no stomach judging by the thinness of his waist. Leo just wanted to shoot him there and then because he was a disgrace to humanity. Leo had already memorised all the crimes of the prisoners on this floor and this man's crime was terrorism.

It was one of the more severe crimes on this floor but it was still a crime, and most of the criminals on this floor were simply charged with conspiracy to commit Treachery. So they were planning to kill Empire officials, commit terrorism or they were planning to actually run off with the traitors and join their ranks.

The idiots.

"My Lord," a prison guard said behind him.

Leo slowly turned around with both his guns drawn as he saw a very tall male prison guard with his rifle draw running behind him.

"We have a small problem," the guard said. "The prisoners are all chanting a single phrase. They're all saying *free the Speaker Of The Lord,*"

As soon as the guard said that Leo knew that something bad was going on because that was the phrase or term used to describe the woman that Inquisitor Mason wanted at all costs. The woman was a strange Speaker to the traitor forces in the Empire.

Apparently she had such a way of speaking to the

masses that she could convert entire Empire Army units to the traitor forces within minutes. Leo had heard the woman speak and that seemed to be impossible but Mason clearly believed differently.

And it was even worse that the little Speaker had already converted two entire worlds to the traitor's cause. There had been full-on rebellions against Empire rule on those planets and eventually the Speaker was captured and now Leo had to bring her to his Master.

But why did the other prisoners want her released when they didn't even know she was here in the first place?

"My Lord," a female voice said over Leo's communication device that was implanted in his ear. "There are twenty ships heading straight for us. I tried to contact for reinforcements but my signals are not working. I tried the emergency Inquisitorial code you gave me and that is not working,"

"Shit," Leo said.

That Inquisitorial code had the power to highjack entire computer networks in an effort to get out an emergency help signal. Whatever technology those twenty traitor ships were using it was so advance that Leo couldn't even imagine what it was.

"Shit. My crew. They're traitors. Fuck," the woman said as a bullet screamed through the air and the line went dead.

A Guard tackled Leo to the ground. Leo snapped his neck. The idiot.

An immense explosion ripped through the ship. Red flashing warning lights appeared on. And all the thousands of prisoners on this floor chanted that Leo was about to die.

And he didn't think they were wrong for a single moment.

CHAPTER 3

Sebastian really hated being trapped in that damn prison cell and the damn icy coldness of his bed was seriously starting to annoy him. Yet the sound of the prisoners shouting, chanting and cackling only made Sebastian's stomach tighten into a painful knot. This wasn't normal for prison ships, but it was normal for traitors that were about to do something very bad.

Sebastian stood up for the first time in ages and he cursed at himself as his knees and legs ached a little. He walked on the spot for a few moments to help get the blood pumping to them.

He had been Empire Army for ages. He should have known not to sit for too long just in case he needed to spring into action quickly and effectively and on extremely short notice.

Thankfully after a few seconds the aching was gone and Sebastian felt fighting fit, but he still couldn't understand what the traitors were so excited about. All the other prisoners were chanting, banging on the steel bars of their prison cells and shouting various treacherous words into the air.

Sebastian tried to look up and down the corridor but the bars restricted his view too much. None of this made any sense whatsoever and it was even stranger that no security measures were kicking in.

If Sebastian had learnt anything from his time dating (and mostly having sex) with an Arbiter was that whenever there was something even remotely looking like a riot on a prison ship was happening. Toxic gas would be pumped into the corridor at all speed, that thankfully wasn't happening. But why?

There was a very hot Inquisitorial Agent on board so clearly that woman whoever she was a highly valuable target. Why wasn't she on a floor all by herself?

"I told you your death was coming," the woman shouted towards Sebastian, and Sebastian really didn't like the weird deranged look in the woman's eyes.

Then Sebastian smiled as three Prison Guards in their strong black uniforms stormed down the corridor towards the woman's cell. Sebastian was relieved that the prison guards were finally going to do something with her.

Then Sebastian noticed that the mark of the Emperor showing their loyalty to him on their uniforms had been ripped off. And the eyes of the prison guards were almost glassy, like they were possessed or something and their hands were burnt and scarred.

Sebastian just shook his head because he had seen those markings before on the jungle world he was fighting on. There was a minor belief amongst Empire forces that the traitors had access to a device that if you stuck it against the head of a loyal soldier for a moment, it would corrupt their mind and turn them into a mindless traitor drone.

Of course loyal soldiers always fought back but the machine was so hot that it burnt their hands. Clearly the device was real, dangerous and now Sebastian's stomach twisted even more.

"Access denied," a computerised voice said as the prison guards tried to open the woman's cell.

An immense explosion ripped through the entire ship and Sebastian gripped the steel bars of his prison cell for support.

Red flashing lights appeared and Sebastian's eyes widened when he saw that the prison guards were now attaching bombs to the woman's prison cell. They were going to blow her out.

It was reasonable to assume that a traitor warship or fighter or something had crashed into the prison ship and caused the other explosion but Sebastian really wanted to stop the woman from escaping.

"Inquisitor!" Sebastian shouted in some vain hope that single powerful word might cut through the shouts in the ears of that hot man.

Everyone laughed at him and Sebastian really hoped that his plan would work because if not, then he was a dead man.

The explosion ripped through the corridor.

Throwing Sebastian against the solid steel wall of his prison cell and Sebastian stared in horror as the steel bars of his own cell were ripped open.

But the smouldering remains of other prisoners filled his senses, Sebastian forced himself to take a few steps forward and he was horrified to see that the woman was now free.

All the prisoners, prison guards and everything else, except him in a ten-cell radius was dead because of the explosion. And even the woman seemed surprised to see Sebastian was still alive but he just looked at her.

"My friends will be raiding the ship within seconds. I suggest you pick up a guard's gun and fight your way off the ship. You cannot come with me but I respect your strength,"

Sebastian was so damn tempted to shoot her there and then but he just couldn't. Then he changed his mind.

Sebastian shot forward. Grabbed a guard's gun and fired it at the woman.

The woman laughed as the bullets simply bounced straight off her and Sebastian noticed the slight glimmer of a personal shield generator around her.

The woman kept walking away. "Did you really think my friends wouldn't protect me?"

Sebastian spat at her direction.

"Oh," the woman said. "And your time is up,"

Sebastian had no idea what she was talking about until a loud deafening alarm screamed overhead and Sebastian just cursed himself as he realised that was the alarm that opened every single prison cell on the ship. Let alone this floor.

Sebastian just stared in utter horror as he saw the steel bars of every prison cell dissolve away and the traitors in them stepped forward. Laughing manically at their new found freedom.

And Sebastian had no friends, no allies and only a single gun against them all.

He really liked those odds.

CHAPTER 4

It had been an absolute nightmare for Leo as he carefully stalked the long, grey metal halls of the prison ship to keep ahead of the ever-escaping traitor forces. He had no idea what in the Emperor's name had happened by there was no end to these traitor forces it turned out.

Leo entered a small hangar that could still easily fit about twenty blade-like transport shuttles, but it was empty. Its walls were perfectly smooth in an ugly grey shade and there were no crates or cover in the entire hangar.

The very fact that there was no cover whatsoever was annoying as hell. Leo loved having cover and it always gave him some kind of tactical advantage but all he needed to do was out flank the traitors and the escaped criminals, get back to the prison cell containing the woman and escape with her.

That was the plan.

The immense smell of smouldering bodies,

charred flesh and burnt gunpowder filled the air of the hangar and Leo knew that the traitors were close. It was clear that some of the prison guards were traitor themselves but it was impossible that they had been traitors before.

He had personally vetted and re-vetted everyone aboard the ship, so that damn woman must have spoken to them one by one and convinced them that she was a divine being that could gift them the galaxy.

It was so damn stupid that so many people believed that simple lie of hers and once she had spoken that lie, they always tended to be more willing and susceptible to the other lies of hers.

Damn the bitch.

Leo quickly realised that he had gotten it all wrong and that the woman was probably gone now and the traitors were clearing the ship of all survivors. At least that way if and when anyone showed up to investigate the slaughter no one would be able to tell them what happened.

Those foul traitors had really thought of everything. Leo knew his only hope was to make it to the main hangar, grab a transport and meet up with the cloaked Inquisitorial warship.

Unless they teleported onboard and saved him first.

"In here I heard something," a man said.

Leo looked for cover but there wasn't any. Leo whipped out his two guns and pointed them in the direction of the voice.

Two short men came in through a large metal doorway and jumped when they saw him.

Leo fired.

One man's head exploded. The other man jumped to one side. He whipped out his gun.

Leo fired.

Bullets screamed through the air. Killing the man. It wouldn't take the enemy long to come and check on the bullet sounds.

Leo had to move now but he really wanted to check in with his friends on the cloaked warships. Just to see if they were at least aware of the situation.

"This is Leo calling *Emperor's Hammer*. Respond," Leo said loudly enough for his communication implant to realise it was a command but quiet enough so the traitors could hear it and come to investigate.

Static filled the line.

"This is Inquisitorial Agent Leo Dawson. Respond *Emperor's Hammer*,"

"What's that noise?" a woman asked in the distance.

Leo cut the line and went over to the massive metal doorway in the direction the noise had come from. He really didn't need this. Even when he was former Empire Army elites he always had five other hot men with him for backup.

"Contact found," a woman said.

The metal wall exploded open where Leo was hiding.

Someone ripped through it. Tackling Leo to the

ground.

The woman slammed her fists into Leo's face. She kept doing it. Rapidly.

Leo tried to block her. The traitor was good.

Leo rolled sideways. Throwing her off him.

Leo jumped up and shot her in the head. She was a young woman maybe no older than thirty but her blackened teeth, scars and slices in her flesh told him she had been a member of the traitors for maybe a decade or more.

Bullets screamed through the air.

Leo rolled to one side.

Five traitor soldiers stormed in. Firing at Leo. He dodged them as much as he could.

More soldiers' footsteps came up behind him.

Loyal prison guards fired. The traitors exploded.

More traitors poured in.

Leo dashed over to the prison guards. Traitor bullets roared towards them.

Slaughtering the guards. Knives flew through the air.

Knives slashed at Leo. He fell to the ground. More knives stabbed around him. Pinning him to the ground.

Then Leo just frowned as he saw the Speaker of Truth walk over to him in all her foul ugliness. She smiled at him and Leo wanted nothing more in that moment than to simply burnt her long black hair.

"Leave this one alive. The knives have him pinned down. When the engines overload, he will learn the true meaning of pain," she said.

As Leo listened to her and the other traitors walk away, he pulled harder and harder against his own battle armour and the knives that pinned him to the ground.

He knew that one of the knife throwers at least had to be a traitor superhuman Angel of Death and Hope to have the required strength to ram a knife through a metal floor. And that only made the Speaker even more dangerous.

The knives weren't moving a millimetre. And Leo realised that he was trapped and was probably going to die here.

Not exactly the way he ever wanted to go out.

CHAPTER 5

Sebastian had actually managed to surprise himself as he ever so carefully stalked the immense ugly grey metal corridors of the prison ship. He had managed to overrun most of the traitors when they had all been unleashed and he supposed that the shouting, screaming and chanting of the prisoners in a ten-cell radius had managed to drown out his call for an Inquisitor.

So as far as the other criminals were concerned he was just another freed criminal like them.

Of course that had all changed now because that stupid woman had managed to somehow corrupt them and now every single criminal on this ship was hunting down those loyal to the Emperor. Sebastian had already managed to kill twenty of them but this wasn't what he needed.

Sebastian just needed to escape this prison ship and get as far away from this awful place as possible. And as much as it seriously annoyed him, Sebastian really wanted that hot man to be okay.

If he ever saw the hot man again, the hottie would probably kill him for escaping the prison cell but Sebastian didn't care. He was loyal to the Emperor and that was all that mattered to him.

Sebastian continued to stalk down a particularly long metal corridor and he was disgusted by the absolutely horrific stunk of rotting flesh, mouldy food and the aroma of charred corpses that just made him want to gag. Clearly all the enviro-systems had shut down on the ship because they normally got rid of the smell so Sebastian hated to imagine how far the corruption spread on the ship.

Someone shouted up ahead.

Sebastian couldn't be certain what was said but he was fairly sure that the person shouting wasn't shouting words. He was shouting pain and shouting because he was in agony.

Sebastian went towards the sound but heard the heavy footsteps of someone behind him.

He spun around. Sebastian shot two criminals in the chest.

Sebastian stopped for a moment. Three more traitors stormed towards him.

Sebastian shot two. Another criminal swung an axe at him. Sebastian ducked.

Sebastian dashed forward. Getting behind the criminal. Sebastian snapped his neck.

Sebastian carefully continued to go towards the sound and was a little surprised that the sound was coming from a small hangar without anything inside it.

There was a man pinned down with knives on the ground but none of them appeared to penetrate the man's fit battle armour.

Sebastian realised that this was the hot man he had seen earlier. The man's guns were centimetres away from his hands but the knives prevented him from getting them. At least the hot man couldn't kill him yet, but he really was beautiful.

His bright red eyes were stunningly beautiful, his face was handsome and smooth and the man's body was perfect.

"What? You gonna kill me criminal," the hot man asked.

Sebastian just shook his head. He was loyal to the Emperor, the Empire and the values of the Empire Army, and there was no way in hell that Sebastian was ever going to leave a follow loyal servant of the Emperor behind.

It might have been stupid to free a hot man that wanted to kill Sebastian for treachery but Sebastian was a servant of the Emperor first and foremost. He pulled all the knives out of the hot man's armour.

The hot man didn't move. He simply stared at Sebastian for a few moments and Sebastian really liked looking into the deep bright red eyes of the hottie.

"You said you were loyal to the Emperor," the hot man said.

Sebastian nodded. "I took my oath to serve Him and I will always honour it,"

The sound of tens upon tens of criminals echoed around the small hangar. Sebastian saw tons of criminals charging towards them in both directions.

"Prove your loyalty!" the hot man said picking up his two guns.

Sebastian went back to back with him and he fired at the enemy.

Bullets screamed through the air. These criminals only carried hammers and bars.

Heads exploded. Sebastian kept firing. More enemies died.

There were so many of them. Sebastian dashed forward.

Pounding his fists into heads. Breaking jaws. Breaking skulls. Snapping necks.

He had to protect the hot man. He was his only chance of freedom.

The hot man hissed.

A steel bar smashed Sebastian in the chest.

He fell to the ground.

The criminals stomped their feet on him.

Sebastian tried to fight back. He couldn't. There were too many of them.

Blue smoke filled the hangar. Machine gun fired through the air. Flames roared overhead.

The hot man grabbed Sebastian by the shoulders and pulled him up. Sebastian noticed there were more heavily armed and armoured men and women in the chamber now.

They must have teleported in.

"Leo," a woman shouted. "We leave now. Ship about to explode,"

"We take this criminal with us. The woman focused on him. He might be useful,"

"Fine!" a man shouted clearly not happy.

Sebastian really wasn't sure if he wanted to go with all these people but it was better than dying a traitorous criminal and getting burnt alive in a ship explosion.

Sebastian nodded. The hot man grabbed Sebastian and blue smoke engulfed them as they teleported away.

CHAPTER 6

As Leo stood in the middle of the large semi-spherical chamber that was the bridge in the very heart of the Inquisitorial Warship *Emperor's Hammer*, he really couldn't believe how badly that mission had gone and it was hardly going to get any better when the others came in for their meeting, and even the criminal was meant to be joining them.

The entire bridge was probably the weirdest in the entire Empire because most normal bridges were rather beautiful with their tiers upon tiers of holographic computers and command crew and the floor-to-ceiling windows that allowed its captains to look out over the vastness of space in real time.

But because the *Emperor's Hammer* was a special warship it was very different, Leo still wasn't sure if he liked the bridge being in the very heart of the ship. It protected the bridge better, of course, but it only meant that Leo didn't get to see the beautiful views of the galaxy when he was in here alone.

In fact there was nothing in the bridge at all besides its smooth grey metal walls that could show a 360-view of the warship with a simple flick of the hand using holograms, there weren't any seats or controls, and there was only a baby blue metal table in the middle of the bridge. That could be activated and it would show tons of holograms depending on what the user wanted.

Leo would so be lying if he said he didn't like that little feature, but the views were his true love.

Leo had always loved those views and there was just something so magical, special and even a little mystical about floating in space with all the stars and delightful planets around you. Ever since he was a child he had always wanted to go out amongst the stars, of course Leo had never intended to serve the Empire Army elite units and then the Inquisition but he wouldn't change his life for anything.

He loved it.

The sound of the metal circular door opening made him smile as Quinn walked in wearing her black battle armour and her heavy flamer was still in her hands, like she was about to be attacked at any moment. Maybe they would be so Leo placed his hands carefully on his two guns on his waist.

Then Marvin stepped into view and he started working on the metal table and activated blue holograms of the system they were in. Marvin was a rather attractive man with his scarred face, muscular body and his killer smile but he was as straight as they came sadly.

His official job for Inquisitor Mason was to run the ship, which he did brilliantly but Leo also really respected him as a friend, battle brother and he was very handy with a machine gun.

"Your criminal is waiting outside with a shock collar around his neck," Marvin said like it was nothing.

Leo almost wanted to tell him off because the criminal wasn't a danger to them but that was only anger and lust and no Agent never acted by emotion. They had to be logical to protect the Emperor and after all, putting a criminal in a shock collar with little bombs inside was Inquisitorial protocol.

"You doubt me for bringing him aboard, don't you?" Leo asked Marvin.

Marvin grinned as he focused on the wreckage of the exploded prison ship as it appeared in holographic form.

"Of course," Marvin said. "You said that the criminal saved you which means you are not as capable as you once were. It was your job to bring the prisoner to Mason and you failed,"

"We were attacked…" Leo started to say but the words died out in his mouth because he knew that there were no excuses in service to the Emperor. And to be honest, there were a number of options Leo could have done to help protect the target even more.

An isolated cell being the easiest and most common sense option.

"He's in a shock collar so if he is a traitor then kill him when he makes his move, but he claims to be loyal to the Emperor and right now there is more evidence supporting that then not," Leo said with a lot more force than he intended to.

Marvin nodded and thankfully Quinn hugged Leo lightly.

"Come in," Leo said so his communication implant could transmit his words to the shock collar and the criminal.

A few moments later the criminal, that Leo now knew was called Sebastian, came into the bridge and stood at attention next to Leo.

Leo was actually shocked. This was the first time he had gotten a real chance to look at the criminal and he was hot. Like really damn hot. In the black robes that Marvin had given him, he looked so fit, slim and downright sexy that Leo felt his wayward parts flare to life.

It would have hardly surprised Leo if Sebastian had a six-pack and v-cut abs, and it was clear from how he was standing at attention he was a former Empire Army something. He had read about all the prisoners earlier but Sebastian's details didn't quite register with him at the moment.

But Sebastian was extremely hot.

"We managed to see that the Speaker escaped on one of the eighteen remaining traitor warships that attacked the prison ship," Quinn said as the hologram zoomed out to show the fleet moving away from them and the wreckage.

"We also know that the woman was able to corrupt loyal prison guards and an entire damn ship," Marvin said.

Leo hated hearing that. It was just so awful that one woman had the power to do that. No one should.

"Our mission is simple. This is a retrieval operation. We need to get the Speaker back into custody so Lord Mason can interrogate her," Quinn said.

Leo nodded and was surprised when Sebastian did. He was clearly focusing on this briefing like he was a normal Empire Army soldier again receiving new orders. Maybe he wasn't a traitor after all.

"Where do we believe they're heading?" Leo asked.

Marvin stayed silent and Quinn actually shrugged so Leo pinched his fingers together and that zoomed the hologram out.

Leo swiped in the direction the traitors were heading and realised that one ship was breaking off from the rest of the fleet. Leo flicked his wrists and the ship's trajectory appeared as a line.

It looked as if the ship that breaking off was heading towards a solar system that was weakly inhabited. There might have only been twenty thousand people in the entire solar system.

There was no way there would be any real Empire Army detachment, Angels or anything to form a defence of the system except from the

Planetary Defence Forces. It was only strange that a single ship was heading for it.

"We need to follow the ship," Leo said.

Marvin cocked his head. "We could but what about the other 17 ships. This could be a diversion or something. The Speaker could still be in that fleet,"

Quinn cursed as more and more ships broke off from the traitor fleet and headed in all sorts of weird and wonderful directions.

Leo slammed his fists into the metal table. It didn't do any damage but it wasn't meant to.

"Permission to speak," Sebastian said like he really was back in the Army.

"Denied Criminal abomination," Marvin said.

"What?" Leo asked trying not to look into the beautiful whiskey-coloured eyes of Sebastian.

"We do as Lord Leo suggested," Sebastian said carefully. "The Speaker will head to a system where she can speak and get more followers for her cause then she can make a new plan to escape whilst she has an entire system to protect her. None of the other ships seem to be heading for a solar system nearby,"

Leo nodded. It made perfect sense and that was similar to how the Speaker operated before.

"I agree," Quinn said but she pulled a gun out on Sebastian. "But how don't we know the Speaker told you to say that to us?"

Leo didn't dare react to this situation. He couldn't openly defend a possible traitor. That would be a death sentence.

Sebastian bowed his head. "I am loyal to the throne and the Emperor and you have a damn shock collar attached to my throat so if you actually believe I am a traitor then kill me,"

Marvin laughed and shook his head. "We keep him alive for now. He's got fight in him,"

Leo weakly smiled because as hot as Sebastian was he just knew that he couldn't keep Sebastian alive for much longer against the suspicions of Marvin and Quinn.

And the very idea of that made Leo a lot more uncomfortable than an Agent ever should have felt for a mere criminal.

CHAPTER 7

Considering that the Inquisition was meant to be a cold, awful and murderous top-secret organisation, Sebastian was actually surprised at how much he enjoyed the next three days with the crew on the *Emperor's Hammer*. The crew were really sweet, funny and they definitely knew how to have a good time, all whilst getting their work done of course.

And as Sebastian sat in the little silver metal quarters that the idiot Marvin had "gifted" him, he just had to admit that it was far, far better than the prison cell he had called home for so long.

The quarters itself was definitely a former storage room. It was barely large enough for Sebastian to lay down in and if Sebastian had any personal items he wanted to lay out in the room and decorate, then there would have been no room for them. Yet at least it didn't smell of poo, wee and other foul smells like the prison ship did.

In fact the only item that Sebastian had had

enough courage to ask beautiful Leo for was a picture of the Emperor.

Back in his Empire Army quarters, Sebastian had always had a picture of the Emperor ever since he had gone to the academy because the Emperor was his Lord and Master and Protector. And it would be a little silly if Sebastian spoke his Oaths into the air at night without directing them at something like a picture.

So Sebastian was more than grateful to sexy Leo as he stared at the little blue holo-image of the Emperor after some battle that was forgotten to history, but Sebastian loved the photo all the same. And the only problem with being here on the *Emperor's Hammer* was the damn shock collar attached to his neck.

Sebastian actually didn't mind protocol in the slightest but the damn collar was massive and it was impossible not to feel it. The rough cold metal against his neck felt strange, annoying and Sebastian just wanted to rip it off. Yet Sebastian knew that if he touched it then the collar would transmit a signal to Marvin and then if Marvin wanted to, he could just electrocute Sebastian.

Hell Sebastian had done that to prisoners before.

Someone knocked on the door and Sebastian grinned when he saw it was beautiful Leo wearing his battle armour, one of his hands was resting on his pistols that hung from his waist. Sebastian was starting to wonder if Leo ever stopped touching them.

He probably didn't and that was wise considering their job.

"We'll arrive in the target solar system in two hours in case you wanted to get ready," Leo said with caring in his voice.

It was rather strange to hear an Agent of the Inquisition actually caring about someone else, but Sebastian really liked it. Well, he really liked Leo anyway and judging by the way that Leo was looking at him with his beautiful bright red eyes he really liked him back.

It was just a sad fact that for now at least they couldn't do anything about it. Sebastian hated the fact that he was still a prisoner and Leo was a sexy hunk of a man that couldn't be a criminal or prisoner. It was only by getting his freedom could Sebastian ever hope to at least ask out the beautiful man in front of him.

"How did you become an Agent?" Sebastian asked.

Out of all the questions, conversations and laughter they had shared over the past three days, Sebastian was actually surprised he hadn't asked that until now.

Leo grinned slightly. "I was a former Empire Army elite trooper as you know. I was stationed on the planet Giga 9-2 during the Purge of Ra and the traitors overwhelmed the planet within hours. Yet I killed my captain when he fell to corruption and I took over my unit. I became a resistance leader,"

Sebastian nodded. "I heard and read battle reports of the Purge. There was a man that single-handedly led the resistance and sabotage operations against the traitors until Empire reinforcements could break through,"

"I couldn't exactly call it single-handed but I liked to think that my actions made a difference to the system,"

Sebastian laughed. "A difference? Without you Empire forces couldn't possibly breach the system and reclaim it in the Emperor's Glory,"

It was so great to know that he was in the presence of a true war hero. Sebastian had wondered for decades who the man actually was but it was clear now that Leo's identity had been erased from official records when he became an Agent of the Inquisition.

"Then after Empire Forces broke through and I helped them reclaim the planet I was trapped on I met Inquisitor Mason. He was the one that led the Empire attack that crippled the enemy resistance I weakened. He liked me, I liked him and he recruited me,"

"I'm glad he did," Sebastian said out of instinct.

"I'll see if Marvin and Quinn will allow you to have some armour for the mission. Meet us in the bridge in an hour for a briefing before we make planetfall,"

"Thank you," Sebastian said.

Leo grinned beautifully and Sebastian really

wanted to see that smile more and more but he just knew where they were going. There wouldn't be a reason to smile for a long time because this Speaker wasn't normal, sane or friendly in the slightest.

And if Sebastian saw her then he knew that she would kill him this time. Or try to at least.

And the very idea of fighting an enemy of the Emperor made him so excited that he was surprised he wasn't bouncing off the walls.

CHAPTER 8

As Leo stood in the large semi-spherical bridge with its walls now showing a wonderful 360-view of the space around the *Emperor's Hammer*, he couldn't believe how much the past two hours had dragged since he had left wonderful Sebastian. Leo had never ever felt like this towards a man before and it was so odd that time just seemed to go faster around him.

And Leo absolutely loved spending time with him.

Leo gently rested both his hands on his two guns on his waist as Marvin, his heavy machine gun hanging from his waist, stood next to him examining the latest data on the grey holographic table as the hologram showed where the Speaker's ship had travelled to.

The air smelt great of strong coffee, peanut cookies that Quinn had cooked especially for them (but not for Sebastian) and the rich sweet aroma of vanilla milkshakes thankfully filled the air. Leo really loved being on the *Emperor's Hammer* because he never could have gotten these delights on a normal Empire Army warship.

The metal door opened behind them and Leo forced himself not to look too excited when he saw Sebastian walk in and stand opposite him. Sebastian might have been wearing paper-thin black battle armour but he was still beautiful.

It was just a shame that Leo couldn't convince Marvin and Quinn to allow the so-called criminal to have a low-velocity gun at the very least. The best weapon they would allow Sebastian to have was a rusty pipe but Leo still loved his best friends all the same.

"Marvin," Leo said focusing on the hologram and wiping his hands so the hologram would zoom in on their target planet. "The Speaker's ship docked an hour ago at this space station,"

Everyone huffed and Leo couldn't blame them as they all focused on a grey space station that looked like a snake moving around the small red planet below. The space station wasn't human-made and that meant that there were aliens in the system.

Leo hadn't read anything about alien sightings in this region of space but this wasn't exactly the busiest of regions so it wasn't like there were a ton of witnesses to report aliens.

"Running the space system design through the database now," Quinn said.

Leo nodded, at least that would allow them to

know exactly what species they were dealing with.

"I've sent reports to Lord Mason," Marvin said. "I think we need to presume that the system has already fallen to the Speaker,"

As much as Leo wanted to disagree because the Speaker had only been in the system for an hour, he knew that it was the safest assumption to have. The Speaker had corrupted entire solar systems in a week or two but that was for systems with a population in the billions and this system only had a population of twenty thousand.

"We need to bring the *Emperor's Hammer* in quick and fast," Sebastian said. "Teleport two people on board, grab the target and get away as fast as possible,"

The entire bridge fell silent.

"And who made you in charge," Marvin said bitterly. "You are a criminal and I doubt your belief in the Emperor first of all. Let alone my belief in your corruption because the Speaker spoke to you,"

Leo watched Sebastian for a moment and he was surprised to see him weighing up something in his mind. Leo wanted to go over to him and place his hand on his but that would hardly look good in front of his friends.

"I want to be honest with you all even if it kills me," Sebastian said, "but I think the Speaker is a bit scared of me. She spoke to me twice on the prison ship and when the bomb went off that killed everyone in a ten-cell radius she was surprised that I was still alive,"

Leo really wished he hadn't of revealed that so publicly but it was good to see Quinn nod at least. Maybe she believed Sebastian wasn't a traitor.

Marvin hummed for a few seconds. "My question is why didn't she die if the explosion was that deadly?"

Leo shrugged but the hologram on the table flashed a few times and Leo noticed the space system was powering down.

The walls of the bridge beeped and Quinn went over to them as the database had found what alien species the space system belonged to.

"The Serpentine Empire is here," Quinn said, "and it looks like the space system is a wreckage that was previously tagged by the Inquisition. I've updated the records,"

Leo bit his lip. This wasn't exactly good but in this line of work he wasn't sure what was good these days. The Serpentine Empire were an alien race made up of immense ten-metre-long snakes that were running across the galaxy after their Empire had mysteriously fallen in the past hundred thousand years.

It was beyond rare for them to come into contact with humanity but these were desperate times for all species, not just the Serpentine.

"Have they made planetfall?" Marvin asked.

Leo shook his head. "And my question is why is the Speaker docking on an alien space station? She must know that the station isn't human,"

Quinn stomped her foot. "She would know and I bet she wants to corrupt the Serpentine,"

Damn it. Leo really hated the notion of the Speaker not only having traitor soldiers and superhumans under her command but also ten-metre snakes. That wasn't a pleasant idea and that would only make her more and more dangerous.

Leo had to stop her no matter the cost.

And Leo really had to force the fact out of his head that no human that went to fight the serpentine ever returned to tell the tale.

CHAPTER 9

Sebastian and beautiful Leo rematerialised into a grey square corridor that curved to the left and Sebastian really hated the foul smell of death, snakeskin and rot. It was an awful smell that clung to the air and the walls like its life depended on it, and Sebastian wouldn't have been surprised if by the time the mission was that the smells clung to him as well.

The damn shock collar zapped him a little and hummed for a few seconds before it went silent and Sebastian was so looking forward to having it off when he earned his freedom.

Leo went ahead a little and Sebastian didn't like the grey metal walls of the corridor much because it looked slightly off. This workmanship was certainly human in nature but yet the database said this was an alien ship.

Something had to be wrong.

Footsteps pounded behind them. Sebastian spun around and a man just stopped in front of them.

The man wasn't wearing any clothes and Sebastian really wished that he had been because the man wasn't attractive in the slightest. So Sebastian raised his rusty metal pipe a little in case he was a danger.

"They're coming," the man said.

Sebastian went forward towards the man and Leo joined him, and as far as Sebastian was concerned this man was an enemy threat.

Something shot towards him. Chomping on the man. The man's body crackled like an egg.

Sebastian's eyes widened when he saw that the thing chomping on the man was an immense red ten-metre-long snake with two very long fangs dripping with the man's dark red blood.

Sebastian stepped slowly back and really wished he had a damn gun.

"*Emperor's Hammer* do you copy?" Leo slowly asked his communication implant.

"I am deeply sorry by dearest Leo," the Speaker said, "but the *Emperor's Hammer* cannot be reached at this time. If you want to leave a message please speak after the tone,"

Sebastian just grinned because the Speaker had style but they were trapped here. And how the hell the Speaker managed to interfere with Inquisitorial technology was beyond him.

The snake looked at Sebastian and his heart pounded in his chest.

The snake charged forward.

Sebastian leapt to one side. The snake zoomed past. Sebastian smashed his pipe on the beast.

The pipe shattered.

The snake slammed Sebastian against a wall. Winding him. Sebastian punched his chest. Air rushed back in.

Leo shot at the snake. The snake shot forward. Diving at Leo.

Sebastian jumped on the snake.

Its scales were ice. Sebastian climbed forward.

The snake jumped up.

Sebastian leapt off the snake. The snake pounded into the ceiling.

Cracking it. Three shards of metal embedded itself in the scales.

Leo kept shooting.

Sebastian punched the snake. Hard. The impact hurt his hand.

It did nothing to the snake. The snake spun around. Launching itself at him.

Leo threw one of his guns at Sebastian. He caught it.

Sebastian aimed at the creature's eyes. He fired.

One eye went up in smoke.

Sebastian fired again.

The other eye burnt away and the snake collapsed on the ground. It was slashing and lashing and pounding itself into the walls.

The walls started to crack.

Sebastian grabbed Leo and charged up the

corridor. It was only a matter of time before the snake broke the walls. Possibly creating an opening into space.

Sebastian kept running.

A wall snapped by the snake.

Sebastian saw a blast door ahead of them. All Sebastian needed to do was get there before the wall snapped completely and the snake was sucked out into space.

A deafening bomb screamed overhead.

Sebastian ran even faster.

The blast door started to shut. It only did that if there was a breach in the corridor.

Leo rushed past him. He made it to the door. Sebastian was almost there.

The force of the vacuum of space threw him backwards. Sebastian struggled to breathe.

Sebastian was hit in the face by a rope of some kind. Sebastian grabbed it.

Leo pulled him to safety and Sebastian was surprised when he entered an oxygen bubble so that's how Leo had managed to pull him to safety without being affected by the lack of air.

"That was close," Leo said as the blast door shut behind them.

"I agree," the Speaker said using the station's intercom system. "I wish you two could have gotten here sooner but my plan worked,"

Sebastian cursed under his breath and his stomach twisted in pain.

"I of course wished Marvin and Quinn were on the station as well but it will not be hard to calculate the cloaked position of the *Emperor's Hammer*. Then I will kill them. I would have liked to know you better but it's shame you're going to die now,"

Sebastian had no clue what she was talking about as the entire station jerked slightly as the warship that the Speaker had docked with presumably shot away from the space station.

The station jerked violently.

The Speaker was shooting at the station.

CHAPTER 10

Leo was just stunned at the sheer boldness, stupidity and balls of the Speaker that she had only led them here to kill them. When they all eventually caught up with the Speaker, Leo was more than determined to kill her slowly and painfully for daring to put his friends and sexy Sebastian in mortal danger.

The entire space station jerked as the Speaker kept firing on them and thankfully Leo knew from looking at plans earlier that the space station was strong enough to give them a few minutes.

Leo looked around where they were. The large grey metal room was just that. A room. It wasn't a place with a computer terminal, escape pod or anything inside.

Leo loved how beautiful Sebastian was tapping on the metal walls to check if any of them were hollow but they weren't. Leo had checked that as well.

The ways in and out of the space station was the hangar, ship docking port and the escape pods. All of those options were now cut off for them because of the blast door locking. There was no way out but Leo was glad that he was reasonably calm about it.

They had to find a way out. It was only a matter of time until the entire station exploded or something.

The station jerked a lot hard.

"Why human workmanship?" Sebastian asked as he kept tapping the walls.

Leo clicked his fingers and rested his hand on the gun hanging from his waist. He should have thought about that sooner too. It was weird that the wielding on the station seemed to be human in nature and not alien.

Leo went over to Sebastian but when he heard the metal floor was hollow in a certain place.

Leo went back over to the small patch of flooring and stomped on it harder. It was certainly hollow and Leo just hoped that they could break it down and it could lead to their salvation. And not death.

Sebastian whipped out his gun and aimed it at the patch of flooring. Leo did the same. They both fired as the station jerked so firmly that Sebastian's shot slammed into Leo's lower leg.

Leo hissed in agony as the shot seared his flesh and sliced through his battle armour but at least his shot had destroyed the flooring. There was an old metal tube large enough for them to fit through underneath.

"The snakes must have enslaved some humans to

build the station and the humans added this escape tunnel probably," Sebastian said.

Through the pain Leo nodded. A deafening boom echoed through the station.

They didn't have a choice now. They just had to escape.

Leo and Sebastian jumped down the tunnel and the icy coldness of space burnt Leo's hand. He tried to slow his descend by firmly placing his hands on the sides of the tunnel.

He went faster.

A white light appeared at the bottom. Leo tried to slow down. He couldn't. He was travelling too fast.

Leo could see the white light was a solid metal floor. Travelling at this speed they would both snap their legs if they landed badly.

There was no time to land correctly.

They were going to break their legs. They would be useless after that. They wouldn't be able to escape.

The white light got closer.

Blue smoke wrapped around them. The station exploded. Extreme heat filled the station.

Leo and Sebastian were zapped away. Leo was just glad the others had teleported them away in the nick of time.

But that was way too close for comfort.

CHAPTER 11

Sebastian seriously couldn't believe the pain flooding his neck from the damn shock collar as he and sexy Leo rematerialised in the bridge of the *Emperor's Hammer*. Sebastian had always flat out hated bloody emergency teleportations but wearing a bulky shock collar only made it worse.

Marvin and Quinn had ripped them out of that tunnel and Sebastian's neck really didn't like it.

As Sebastian glared at Marvin and rubbed his neck gently, he had to admit Marvin really didn't seem pleased to see him or maybe that was because beautiful Leo was limping from where Sebastian had accidentally shot him.

Sebastian absolutely hated himself for shooting Leo. He had been the only person on the ship that had actually tried to help, support and protect him from the others, and he had just shot him. That wasn't good at all and Sebastian really hoped that Leo wasn't angry at him.

Quinn helped Leo lean against the grey metal table as she grabbed a medical gun that healed the wound as quickly as it had appeared. Sebastian weakly grinned at the beautiful, clever and kind man that he was starting to fall for.

"So you allowed the prisoner to get a hold of your weapon and he shot you with it," Marvin said resting his hand on his machine gun.

Sebastian noticed that Quinn also had her hands firmly on her flamer.

Leo shook his head and told them exactly how the gun wound had happened but Sebastian could easily tell that Marvin wasn't convinced at all.

"We better get underway before the Speaker starts searching for us," Leo said.

"I agree but what happened to the population?" Sebastian asked then he looked at the spherical walls of the bridge and noticed that in the distance of 360-view of the space around them, there were tons of little dots rising from the planets.

"Damn," Marvin said. "There's ships,"

"Affirmative," Quinn said zooming in on the ships using the hologram on the table in front of all of them. "I'm detecting twenty cruisers,"

"That would be enough for the entire population," Sebastian said. "Do you really think she's good enough to corrupt twenty thousand people in such a short space of time?"

Marvin spat at Sebastian and he really wanted to punch him. "There is nothing *good* about her,"

"We have to leave now," Leo said. "We can fight later but-"

Red flashing lights flashed overhead and a holographic form of the Speaker appeared on the table.

"Finally I have your damn location," the Speaker said through the hologram. "All forces head to these coordinates. I'm uncloaking the ship now,"

"She couldn't," Sebastian said.

"Shit," Marvin said.

The entire ship hummed, popped and vibrated harshly as the cloaking technology exploded and even more warning lights flashed overhead.

Sebastian tried to engage the anti-fire protocols on the ship with Marvin but they weren't working.

The *Emperor's Hammer* shook as the enemy fired upon it.

"Get us out of here!" Leo shouted.

Sebastian looked at Marvin but he shook his head. Marvin couldn't get access to the engines and he had lost control of the ship.

Leo whipped out his guns and ran over to one of the walls of the bridge. He slammed his fist into it and a small section popped out.

Sebastian rushed over to him. There was a large glass cable with blue electricity flowing through it.

Leo shot it and Sebastian tackled him to the ground as lightning shot out.

It zapped Sebastian. It went after a few moments and at least beautiful Leo was okay.

The entire ship went silent for a few moments and the Speaker disappeared from the ship.

"What happened?" Sebastian asked.

Him and Leo jumped back up and Sebastian followed Leo back over to the grey table.

"I deactivated the ship. We have seconds later the Speaker gets over her confusion and starts firing again," Leo said.

Marvin slapped the metal table and it hummed. Three holograms appeared and Sebastian realised they were some kind of emergency power things.

Marvin punched one and the entire ship jerked so hard that Sebastian fell to the ground.

All the ship's systems reactivated and Marvin flew the ship forward with Quinn studying the enemy cruisers.

Sebastian was about to go over to Quinn and help her examine what the twenty cruisers were doing but he noticed there were nineteen traitor warships heading into the system trying to cut them off.

"Emergency slidespace jump now!" Sebastian shouted.

Marvin and Leo and Quinn looked at what he was talking about. Their hands all formed fists. Sebastian just wanted them to do a slidespace jump so they could quickly escape the system.

"Your Speaker master would love that," Marvin said. "She probably uploaded a destination for us,"

Sebastian really hated Marvin.

The entire ship shook violently. Sebastian caught

sexy Leo as he fell.

"Traitor warships preparing to fire cannons. We have to go!" Quinn shouted.

"Fine," Marvin said programming the order. "Let's see what the Speaker has install for us,"

Sebastian was glad they were going to jump away from this fight. The ship turned away from the planets to make the jump safely.

A cruiser smashed into the back of them. The ship turned back towards the planet.

Sebastian screamed as the ship might get caught in the gravitational pull of the planets when they jumped.

The ship zoomed away.

SPEAKER OF TREACHERY

CHAPTER 12

Seconds later a deafening roar ripped through the *Emperor's Hammer* and Leo gripped the metal table so hard that his knuckles turned bright white.

But as he looked at the spherical walls of the bridge, he just smiled that they were away from the enemy and they weren't in another solar system. They seemed to be flowing in-between systems that were largely empty and there wasn't a single other ship nearby.

Leo let out a breath he didn't know he was holding and he was more than glad the emergency jump had worked, but he had been doing this far too long to know that the deafening noise wasn't meant to happen so clearly something had gone wrong.

Leo rested his hands on both his guns and he was just glad that he was okay, safe and with all his friends. Sebastian smiled at him as he stood next to Marvin, it was great to see how in control, calm and collective Sebastian was given the situation.

Most inquisitorial Agents weren't that calm when they first started so it was amazing to know that Sebastian was taking this business really well. And that only made him even more attractive of a stunning man that Leo was fairly sure he had already fallen for him.

"We have three problems," Marvin said looking up for the diagnostic scan he had just run.

Leo rolled his eyes at the situation, not his friends. "What happened?"

"The Speaker left a communication in the ship's data," Sebastian said, "and it's addressed to me personally and most of our port side is scorched. It will take a while for your repairing technology to fix it,"

Leo cursed under his breath. He sometimes forgot how only the inquisition had access to the self-repairing technology that he took for granted, but it was worst that the port side was scorched, probably by scratching against the atmosphere of a planet as they made the jump. It meant that their portside hangars, cannons and guns were out of action.

That seriously limited them in a fight.

"What's the third problem?" Quinn asked.

"The Speaker installed a programme that makes our location transmit itself on traitor frequencies every minute," Marvin said. "I can deactivate it but it will take ten minutes,"

"Let's just hope traitors don't find us in ten minutes. How far did we jump?" Leo asked.

Sebastian laughed. "Three systems over,"

Damn it. Leo had hoped to put a lot more distance between them and the Speaker whilst they regrouped and came up with a plan to actually stop her in her tracks.

Leo went over to Sebastian and he might have been battered, a criminal and someone that his friends wanted to kill at a moment's notice, but he was gorgeous. There was just something so seductive, really cute and alluring about this Empire Army Commander that Leo wanted to kiss him so badly.

He didn't dare do that sadly.

"Play the message please Marvin," Leo said, "whilst you deactivate this transmitting programme,"

Marvin shook his head but did it. Leo hated it as the Speaker's foul face appeared on the metal table and she grinned at them.

"I actually hope you aren't dead so you get to see this little message," the Speaker said. "Yet I want to dangle a little carrot in front of you because I'm heading to the 99th Crimson Station to transmit a little speech of mine,"

Then the hologram buffered.

"And to my dearest Sebastian. I do not understand why you seem to be resistant to my corruption and my explosions but I will find out and if you are still alive, I will kill you,"

Leo was surprised at the Speaker's voice. She was actually annoyed at Sebastian, truly annoyed that he hadn't died like the other prisoners on the prison ship.

Leo paced around the bridge a little because it made no sense. The Speaker was right about it being annoying but it was a good thing because otherwise he also would have died on that prison ship, and he never would have gotten a chance to meet the hottie he was falling for.

Yet it was also strange that Leo didn't feel like the Speaker was using her corrupting powers on them. Because none of them appeared to have fallen under her influence like the twenty thousand people of the last solar system had.

Why?

"What's the 99th Crimson Station?" Sebastian asked.

Leo had completely forgotten that not everyone knew it and judging by the looks on Quinn's and Marvin's faces they had as well.

"It's a little orbital space station in the middle of a heavily protected system," Marvin said. "It absorbs all the incoming and outcoming transmissions in the region,"

Leo just cursed. "That why she wants it. She wants to use it to highjack all transmissions in the region so everyone listens to her speak,"

"And get corrupted," Sebastian said.

Leo really loved how quick Sebastian was getting with all this new information.

Quinn took out her flamer. "Damn the woman. That could lead to billions beyond the region getting corrupted let alone the people in the region,"

"Damn," Sebastian said. "She could make the ships travelling out of the region continue to broadcast her message like a hotspot or traveller speaker beyond the reach of the 99th Crimson Station,"

"It gets worse," Marvin said and Leo had never heard him sound so angry.

Leo watched as Marvin pulled up a map of several sectors of space and their region looked like a drop of an ocean compared to the rest of the sectors. And then a very thin red line appeared heading from their sector to the Sol System.

"An Inquisitorial warship is scheduled to head from this region to Earth in three weeks' time after it's finished giving evidence in a conclave," Marvin said.

Everyone fell completely silent.

Leo focused on all the sectors, regions and solar systems that the warship would have to enter to get to Earth. There were tens or hundreds of billions of people in each system let alone each region of space.

And Leo couldn't focus on anything else except the very idea that the speech would get played in the Sol System itself.

And that realisation hung in the air around them because everyone realised just how threatening this was to the entire Empire.

CHAPTER 13

Sebastian was still surprised how much he enjoyed the next three weeks as the *Emperor's Hammer* travelled towards the 99th Crimson station. He wasn't that surprised that him, sexy Leo and Quinn had been working a lot harder than Sebastian ever thought possible whilst Marvin worked on flying the ship through slidespace (and how to avoid a massive asteroid belt that was in their way) but it had been so much fun.

They had all laughed, joked and told so many fantastic stories to each other that Sebastian was fairly sure he would class all of them as great friends, far better friends than he ever had in the Empire Army.

Because after a month with these amazing people who did the impossible every single day Sebastian realised that he didn't have any friends in the Empire Army. He was in charge of them and that was it. No one wanted to be friends with a Commander and later a criminal.

But here Sebastian actually had friends and a sexy potential boyfriend and that was simply brilliant.

"We're approaching the Station now," Marvin said over the ship's intercom system. "We will arrive at target location in three hours,"

Sebastian was sitting in one of the warship's many bars that was a near-perfect replica to those of old Earth. Sebastian wasn't really a fan of the dark oak walls, little wobbly round tables and the wooden bar that stunk of cheap alcohol.

Sebastian wasn't drinking but he just wanted a few more precious moments with beautiful Leo. The perfect man that he had become really dependent on over the past few weeks and as the damn shock collar hummed in his ears, Sebastian was so looking forward to asking Leo, Marvin and Quinn for his freedom after this mission.

If he survived that was.

"You ready?" Leo asked as he sat next to Sebastian and frowned briefly at the wobbly wooden chair.

"Of course," Sebastian said. "If I die today then it will be an honour to die fighting for the Emperor,"

Sebastian was surprised to see Leo half-smiling because it was a plain and simple truth to him. He was a servant of the Emperor and it was why he had signed up to the Empire Army straight out of school, and there was no higher honour in the Empire than dying in service.

And that wasn't a lie, propaganda or anything. It

was truth.

"Want to know what you were arrested for?" Leo asked just letting the question hang in the air between them.

Sebastian shrugged. "It still won't change anything in the eyes of Marvin and Quinn. The two people who I'm fairly sure will kill me after the mission,"

Leo frowned. "You're one of us as far as Mason is concerned. Only he can give the kill order now that you've spent so much time with us and he won't kill you until he's interrogated you,"

Sebastian really didn't know how that was meant to make him feel better.

"According to an Empire Army soldier, Captain and cleaner under your command they photographed you taking brides with an enemy of the Emperor," Leo said not sounding convinced.

Sebastian bit his lip. "It isn't true but I know who came up with the lies. There was a Captain under my command who wanted me to promote him and he was desperate for it. He had a wife back home but he threw himself at me and I rejected him,"

"Why was he so desperate for the promotion?" Leo asked.

Sebastian weakly smiled because it was going to sound silly to someone as perfect and beautiful as Leo but it wasn't to normal people.

"Back on his wife's home planet a retired Commander was sniffing around her and he was trying to court her. The only hope apparently the captain had of keeping the wife was to become better than a *mere Captain*,"

"Really?"

"It was what I heard so I guess the wife left him and the Captain wanted revenge over me for that. But to be honest the Captain was aggressive and rather foul after a sniff of drink so I doubt it was because of the promotion the wife left,"

Leo slowly nodded and Sebastian just couldn't believe how lucky he was. He was sitting alone with such a hot beautiful man that was far hotter than anyone he ever could have dreamt of.

"We need to go and prepare for the mission," Leo said. "The plan's simple. The Speaker would have only just reached the Station before us so she wouldn't be able to corrupt me. You and me will go in, secure her and return before she has time to do her plan,"

Sebastian just grinned and nodded. "You seriously think it's that easy?"

Leo laughed. "Of course not. But you and me will return, you will be free and you'll be found non-guilty and then you and me can see what we're going to do about our feelings,"

Sebastian just grinned at that idea. There were so many things he wanted to do with and to Leo that he had no idea where to start.

"I'll get my armour on," Sebastian said really wanting to have a more romantic conversation with

Leo when they returned.

"I look forward to it," Leo said.

And Sebastian couldn't agree more.

CHAPTER 14

Leo really had to force himself not to rest his hands on his two guns hanging from his waist as him and wonderful Sebastian stepped out of the storage room that they had teleported into.

They both wore long brown cloaks that were very typical of traders, workers and travellers on stopping off at the 99th Crimson Station for repairs or a quick stop before they got on their way. Leo wasn't a fan of the awful fabric that made the cloaks because the cloaks also gave them little protection against bullets.

It still itched like hell though.

Leo and Sebastian walked through a very long metal corridor with brass-coloured walls and ceiling and floor. The corridor inclined a fair bit so even though the Station was like a massive round disc, the corridor had to be leading them towards the commercial hub in the very heart of the Station.

There were so many people around as Leo glided

through the crowd. There were tons of men and women of all ages and all social classes, but mostly they were all workers stopping off here before they hopped onto their ship taking them to whatever their next planet was in search of work.

It was a sad truth in the Empire that unless you lived on a major hive world, mining world or a planet owned by Mars there just never seemed to be enough jobs.

It was partly why so many people signed up for the Empire Army. It was the only certain way to get shelter, three meals a day (sometimes) and warmth (sometimes it was only bodily warmth but still).

Leo continued going through the crowd and up towards the commercial hub and he didn't like this at all. There were so many people here and they all stunk of burnt oil, wee and illegal stimulants that it was impossible to see if any of them were the Speaker.

"We need to find the communication hub," Sebastian said.

"I agree but we cannot reveal ourselves as the Inquisition for now," Leo said. "It closes as many doors as it opens,"

"How will we find the Speaker then?" Sebastian asked as he stepped out the way for an elderly couple.

"I think she'll find us in the end,"

As much as Leo didn't like that idea he truly believed it. Somehow the Speaker seemed to always know what they were thinking or doing or at least planning. And it seemed to be only through luck recently that they were still alive.

A few moments later Leo and Sebastian reached the top of the corridor and he just frowned as he looked at the Arbiter security measures that formed a large grey metal wall with massive crowds in front of them with only two security points.

It would take hours upon hours for all these people to get through the security measures. And Leo and Sebastian couldn't go through them because of his two guns and Marvin had been nice enough to give Sebastian a metal pipe without a single shred of rust on it.

"We need to go back," Leo said. "We'll find another way around,"

"We cannot. Look," Sebastian said pointing towards the top of the security line.

Leo couldn't believe it. It was the Speaker herself in her black dress, long black hair and foul evil eyes.

Leo whipped out his guns. "Move! Inquisition!"

Leo charged forward but there were too many stupid sluggish people. This wasn't good. Leo had to get to the security chamber now.

The Speaker whipped out a gun. Shooting the security guards in the head.

People screamed. Shouted. Ran away.

Leo fought against an impossible tide of people running towards him. They just kept pushing him further and further back.

Someone knocked Leo to the ground.

People ran over Leo. Other people were knocked

over too. Leo listened to their screams as they were trampled to death.

Leo couldn't move. People kept on stomping on him. Trampling him.

"Inquisition!" someone shouted.

People screamed as something metal smashed into them. Two large hands grabbed Leo pulling him up.

Leo smiled at Sebastian. The man that had just saved his life.

Leo spun around. Looking at the security measures but the Speaker was gone. She had entered the Station.

She was one step closer to getting to the communication hub allowing her to broadcast her speech and damn the Empire.

Leo had to hurry. Time was seriously running out.

CHAPTER 15

Sebastian held his damn metal pipe out in front of him like a sword as he and wonderful Leo went through the 99th Crimson Station's brass-coloured corridors in search of the foul Speaker. Sebastian just knew that she had to be here somewhere.

They only needed to find her.

Sebastian really enjoyed following Leo from behind as it meant he got to look at his great ass as they went towards the communication centre of the Station. It was just a pain whenever Sebastian sadly had to look away from the great sight.

The Station was mainly about monitoring and transmitting all the incoming and outgoing transmissions in the region but there were plenty of other places too. That only made it more difficult to stalk the corridors towards the centre.

After a few moments Sebastian raised his metal pipe a little higher as Leo pointed towards a large solid black wall at the end of the corridor. That wouldn't have bothered a lot of people in the Empire but Sebastian just knew that it was a very clever security measure.

Both of them went over to it and Sebastian was really glad when his damn shock collar seemed to relax a little. Sebastian only noticed it because he felt some kind of absence in the constant humming of the collar.

"Inquisitorial Agent Leo acting on the authority of Inquisitor Mason," Leo said placing his hand against the black wall.

The entire station hummed, banged and popped a little but Sebastian raised his pipe because this felt wrong.

He had heard about these doors before from various agents of the Emperor he had encountered over the years and normally they simply dissolved straight away. Something had changed and in these sort of situations change was never good.

"Could she had gotten through already?" Sebastian asked.

Leo shook his head. "I don't know. This door shouldn't be here now,"

Sebastian heard something crackle behind them. He turned around and was really pleased there was nothing there. But what made the crackling sound?

Leo tackled him to the ground.

A shotgun roared. Sebastian leapt up. Seeing there were ten men with glassy eyes storming out of the door.

They were the damn security guards of the Station. They should be loyal to the Emperor and not working against the Emperor.

Sebastian charged over. Swinging his metal pipe.

Skulls shattered. Blood spattered up walls. Corpses fell to the ground.

Shotguns were fired. Sebastian ducked. Shotgun pellets dug into his armour.

Leo fired. Bullets screaming through the air.

Sebastian charged.

Smashing his pipe into the back of their heads. He had to keep killing. He couldn't allow them to hurt beautiful Leo.

An enemy tackled Sebastian.

Sebastian felt the shotgun barrel press against his shock collar. The collar hummed violently.

Sebastian punched the enemy. Knocking him off. The collar went silent.

Sebastian rammed his pipe into the man's mouth. Forcing it down his throat.

Within minutes all the ten men were dead and Sebastian went over to Leo and just shook his head. This wasn't right in the slightest and he was actually surprised at how relaxed he felt. Mainly because at least they now knew exactly what they were facing more than anything else.

There were no allies on this Station.

Sebastian poked his pipe against the black wall and smiled as the pipe disappeared inside.

Sebastian offered Leo his hand and gestured that

they should walk through the wall together but Leo shook his head.

"We need to battle ready," Leo said.

Sebastian nodded and he stepped through the black wall into pitch darkness. And none of it made sense.

Sebastian couldn't see anything and his heart pounded in his chest. He had no idea where he was, how big the room was or anything. And this felt so so wrong.

A punch came from nowhere. Knocking Sebastian to the ground.

Sebastian went to jump up and swing his pipe but he felt someone put him in a headlock and he shouted as loud as he could for Leo as he saw blue smoke swirl around him.

Someone was trying to teleport him off.

As Sebastian felt the ground fall away from him he just knew he was in deep trouble and danger and beautiful Leo was all alone in a Station filled with people that wanted him dead.

Sebastian hated truly hated that realisation.

CHAPTER 16

As the lights exploded on with a loud crackle Leo cursed under his breath as he saw swirls, twirls and whirls of blue smoke disappear leaving only him standing in a massive sterile white room with six other corridors shooting out from it.

Leo hated this damn bloody Speaker so much that he gripped his two guns so tight that his knuckles turned white. She was so annoying and now he had lost the man he was falling for and to be honest loved.

Leo just had to find Sebastian. He didn't want Sebastian to get hurt, injured or anything.

But Leo forced himself to take a deep breath of the burnt oil-scented air because Sebastian was an Empire Army Commander, he could surely handle some dumbass traitors. And the best way to truly help Sebastian was to find and kill the Speaker before she risked the safety of the Empire.

Leo went forward and went down a perfectly

straight copper-coloured corridor that should take him into the heart of the Station if he was remembering the plans he studied.

Once in the heart of the Station as he really hoping he would be able to find the communication relay that actually controlled the transmissions and how they interacted and connected with the Station itself. Quinn explained it to him as like a Wi-Fi connector that allowed a computer to connect with a network.

If that connector was destroyed then the Speaker simply couldn't transmit anything.

"You think that Agent's coming?" Leo heard a woman ask at the end of the corridor.

"I dunno," a man said.

Leo just smiled as he carefully placed his two guns back on his waist and he grinned at the woman and man standing at the end wearing black uniforms.

"Who are you?" the woman asked Leo.

Leo focused for a moment on the thousands upon thousands of flashing lights set against the smooth black walls covered in servers and other computery things that Leo had no idea about in the room the man and woman were guarding.

Badly guarding.

"The Speaker sent me to check you two were going your job correctly," Leo said.

"I told you you needed to have your communicator on," the woman said.

"And I told you to calm down," the man said

loudly.

Leo whipped out his guns. Shot them both in the head.

Leo went into the room with all the computer servers and other things that he didn't fully understand and a massive golden door slammed down behind him.

And all the flashing lights and black things disappeared revealing only smooth brass-coloured walls.

"It is truly amazing," the Speaker said in Leo's communication implant, "how easy it is to change Station plans to lure you into this trap,"

Leo just grinned because he had to admit he hated the woman but she was bloody clever.

"So I have your boyfriend with me now. I have you trapped and I'm about to take control of the transmission and start broadcasting,"

Leo looked around. He just had to escape. He had to find a way to stop her.

"Oh," the Speaker said, "and I forgot to mention. The room's airtight and I forget to deactivate the fire protocols. Sorry. Not,"

Leo had no idea what she was talking about until a small hole opened in the ceiling opened and a flaming glass bottle smashed down on the floor.

It was a damn petrol bomb. The flames spread across the floor and Leo couldn't put them out.

And if this was like all other Empire Stations. Within moments the air would be sucked out of the room and Leo would die.

He had to escape.

Leo went over to the immense door that trapped him and he was surprised that it wasn't a part of the original Station. The Speaker had this door added in recently.

Meaning it ran on a different system to the rest of the Station and the Speaker had only been here for a few hours so she probably didn't have time to hide the system very well.

Leo started kicking the metal wall around the door in case there was a weak section.

A moment later he kicked through a piece of wood revealing a small computer terminal, wires and a holographic keypad.

A loud hissing filled the air and Leo cursed. The air was being sucked out of the room.

Leo knelt down and took a massive gulp of air.

He tapped the computer terminal. It wanted an override. He didn't know what code she had used to lock the door.

He knew nothing about her. He couldn't possibly make an educated guess. Leo went to breathe but he couldn't breathe in any air.

Leo's lungs screamed out for air. Air that would never come unless he did something.

Leo just hoped this was an Empire-made keypad. He typed in his Inquisitorial ID code and thank the Emperor. The door opened.

He was about to stand up and take wonderful

deep breaths of the burnt-oil-scented air but Leo just frowned when he saw ten women were standing there with machine guns.

He was going to be captured.

CHAPTER 17

Sebastian couldn't believe how stupid the Speaker was as he woke up after being knocked unconscious and found himself standing without resistance in a large circular metal control room. Sebastian hated the pink holographic computers that hugged the walls and there was a small circular raised platform in the middle of the control room.

Sebastian hated the platform because that was the location that would allow the Speaker to transmit her lies, deceptions and manipulations all over the region and eventually the Sol System.

Sebastian couldn't understand for a moment why the stupid Speaker hadn't tied him up or something and the damn humming of the shock collar in his ears was downright annoying.

"Do you like me?" the Speaker asked as she wiped some symbols on the holographic computer she was standing at with her back to him.

"I hate you," Sebastian said taking a few steps

towards her but going slow enough not to seem like a danger to her.

There weren't guards or someone in the control room which was a little confusing.

"You're a traitor to the Emperor. You are a tool of the Lord of War and his superhuman monsters,"

The Speaker laughed. "Do you want to know why I have the power to influence so many minds?"

Sebastian was about to say yes when an oval door opened and Sebastian frowned and his hands formed fists as he saw ten women with machine guns escorting Leo into the control room.

At least beautiful Leo was okay and Sebastian had to force himself not to run over to him and hug him.

"I have the power to influence so many people because the Lord of War made me," the Speaker said as she swiped and typed and even kicked the holographic computer faster and faster.

"Oh damn," Leo said.

Sebastian had no idea what he was so worried about.

"One of the Lord of War's hobbies is creating robots that look identical to humans. There have only been three of these robots ever found but I think this one is a fourth," Leo said.

Sebastian didn't exactly understand what Leo was saying but he couldn't deny how much concern, worry and hate there was in Leo's voice. This was a massive problem.

"At least someone knows what my Master does in his spare time," the Speaker said her voice becoming more mechanical.

Sebastian looked round for his metal pipe but he couldn't see it.

"And you should know," the Speaker said, "the human brain is a device that takes in sound, light and other stimuli and combines it into information,"

Sebastian nodded. It was basic science if not a little oversimplified.

"And my Master gave me an implant that allows me to transmit my speeches at a certain frequency that makes the human mind very suggestible,"

Sebastian just laughed. It sounded so ridiculous but he knew it was true. He had dated a man years ago that worked in a similar area and it was all true. At the right frequency the brain could be forced to believe anything.

"Let me show you Sebastian,"

Sebastian charged at her and the women pressed their machine guns against Leo's head and Sebastian stopped dead in his tracks.

A slight humming and cracking filled the air as the Speaker stared at Sebastian.

"The Emperor is a liar," the Speaker said as her voice echoed in his mind. "The Emperor hates you. You and your friends die each day and he laughs at you,"

Sebastian grinned as images of his friends' bodies being ripped apart, exploding and dying filled his mind. It was so stupid that the Speaker's tricks were working.

"You see the truth. You and your friend die so the Emperor can sit on a throne he never deserved. He gets fatter and fatter by the day whilst you grow weaker,"

Sebastian shook his head. He wasn't listening to this.

"Isn't that right Leo?" the Speaker said.

Sebastian just looked at Leo and his eyes were glassy and he was nodding like a little docile puppy at the Speaker.

Sebastian's heart leapt into his throat as the woman handed Leo back his pistols.

"Kill your boyfriend," the Speaker said.

Sebastian's mouth dropped as Leo charged at him.

CHAPTER 18

Sebastian flat couldn't believe this was happening. It should have been impossible for Leo to turn traitor but clearly the damn Speaker was just that good, or bad to be honest.

Sebastian didn't want to hurt the beautiful love of his life but he also didn't want to die at all. And Sebastian had no idea whatsoever how the hell he was meant to undo the Speaker's bloody influence.

Leo flew at Sebastian.

Sebastian blocked punches. Kicks. Attacks.

Leo was fast. Too fast. He slammed his fists into Sebastian's face.

Pain flooded his senses.

Leo kicked Sebastian in the stomach. Sebastian blocked a punch to his head.

Sebastian whacked Leo across the face. Leo didn't even register it.

He charged at Sebastian. Sebastian leapt to one side.

Sebastian tripped him over. Climbing on top of him.

Leo headbutted Sebastian from behind. Sebastian fell backwards. Leo leapt up.

Kicking Sebastian in-between the legs.

Sebastian stumbled back. His armour was useless.

Leo kicked Sebastian in the chin. A woman got Sebastian in a headlock.

Leo whipped out a gun and aimed.

"Enough," the Speaker said softly still focusing on Leo and immediately Leo put the gun back on his waist.

Sebastian was almost glad about the damn shock collar now because he could feel how badly the woman holding him wanted to strangle him but the shock collar prevented her from closing the headlock around his neck.

That just might be his salvation.

As the Speaker went back to work on her holographic computer and Leo just stared into space like a zombie, Sebastian had to admit she was clever but he had to be smarter. Not only for the sake of the Empire but also for the man he loved.

If the Speaker was a robot and she used a special frequency that made the human brain more susceptible to her influence then there had to be some kind of counter-frequency or something.

Sebastian certainly didn't have any equipment or anything to even begin to create such a frequency. But the brain was easy to manipulate in other ways like if the brain was overloaded and had to shut down then they just might wipe away her influence.

Like if Sebastian whacked Leo over the back of the head.

Sebastian liked that idea but Leo was an Inquisitorial Agent. He wasn't some traitor scum that had no idea. Sebastian just had to try.

"Did you want to know a little secret I learnt about those shock collars?" the Speaker asked as she seemed to be accessing the Station's entire network.

Sebastian stayed silent.

"It turns out that shock collars are designed to be unwearable to those truly loyal to the Emperor. I know it sounds weird but it's true. I've seen loyal members of the Emperor get trapped in them for minutes then the collars simply fall away,"

Sebastian hated that she was implying he wasn't completely loyal to the Emperor. This was probably just another trick of hers.

"It's a pain in the ass for me but, ah here we go," the Speaker said.

The entire Station hummed to life and the raised platform glowed bright white as it presumably connected with every single transmissible system in the entire region and the Inquisitorial ship that was heading to Earth.

"Right… now that I've uploaded by a virus to all these transmitters I now control them," the Speaker said.

Sebastian looked at the ten women with their

machine guns. They were completely distracted. The time to strike was now.

Sebastian stomped on the woman's foot.

She screamed. Sebastian elbowed her in the ribs. Shattering two.

She released him. Sebastian spun around. Heading her in the head.

The woman left backwards. Knocking over two more women.

Sebastian charged to Leo. He was aware.

Leo leapt into the air.

Sebastian ducked. Grabbing Leo's foot. Swinging him about.

Sebastian released him.

Leo flew through the air. Smashing the back of his head on a metal wall. He was out cold.

Women leapt on Sebastian.

Machine guns fire lit up the control room.

Two of the controlled women were awake. They were firing on the enemy.

Sebastian spun around. The Speaker was in the raised platform. A shield had activated around her.

Sebastian charged forward.

Machine gun bullets peppered the ground of him and Sebastian just stopped as five remaining women focused their machine guns on him.

"We will kill you," a woman with red hair said.

Sebastian looked over at Leo who was laying there perfectly still but his eyes were open and they weren't glassy at all.

His Leo was back and now the enemy was going to be slaughtered.

CHAPTER 19

Leo was bloody livid with the stupid pathetic Speaker as he jumped up. How dare she mess with his head and try to make him kill the man he loved. Leo was going to rip her limb from limb for that abominable crime.

Leo threw Sebastian a gun as the five remaining women open fired.

Leo and wonderful Sebastian dashed to the raised platform. Using the Speaker's shield as a barrier between them and the women.

The Speaker shouted her hate and lies and deception. Leo knew it was being transmitted all over the region.

They had to stop it and now.

Leo looked at Sebastian and they both raised their guns.

They charged out of their cover. Firing endlessly.

Machine gun fire roared through the air. The women were awful shots.

Leo fired.

The enemy's heads exploded. Chests gushed with blood. Leo didn't stop.

He stormed forward. Making sure the enemy died. Sebastian did the same.

Within moments all the foul enemy were dead but Leo was a lot more concerned about all the other enemies that were crawling over the station. It wouldn't be long until they had company again.

Leo aimed his gun at the Speaker's shield. He fired. The bullet simply burnt away.

As the Speaker kept talking she grinned at him and all Leo wanted to do in that moment was kill her. Yet the shield protecting her was too strong and he didn't have the firepower to break it.

Or did they?

Sebastian bought over a machine gun each for them and both of them pressed their backs against the wall and they fired.

Leo loved the sound of machine guns firing but all the bullets simply burnt away from the shield like their bullets were made from ice.

"Twenty percentage completion," a computerised voice said.

Leo dashed over to a computer and cursed.

"She's rigged it so her message spreads out like a wave," Leo said. "We need to stop her and the wave,"

"The wave's easy. We just need to create a bigger more powerful shockwave that basically dissolves her corrupting one," Sebastian said.

Leo really loved how smart he was.

Leo went swiped a few times on the holographic computer. "Her ship's still docked. If we disengage it and get the Station to fire on it. The ship's explosion might do the trick,"

Sebastian grinned and Leo understood why. It was a fun plan but they had to deactivate the infuriating shield around her first.

"Inquisitorial Agent Leo wanting shield override," Leo said.

"Access denied. Alerting all allied forces," the computer said.

Leo watched as Sebastian rushed over to the door and smashed the controls. That was the last thing they needed. Leo didn't want the rest of the enemy coming up here.

Then Leo clicked his fingers. The stupid Speaker was a robot at heart and machines were a damn slight more sensitive to frequencies than humans.

Sebastian came over to him. "What you doing?"

Leo swiped on the holographic computers. "We cannot solve this with guns. All Empire stations are rigged with frequency generators in case they were ever attacked by the Robot Created,"

Sebastian laughed and Leo also loved the stories of that robot alien race that once threatened the Empire.

"Ever since that attack the Empire has installed frequency generators in all warships and space stations. I had forgotten until now,"

"Unleash all frequencies," Sebastian said. "Let's see if we can kill her and free the other people too,"

Leo nodded. He set up the frequencies but of course not unleashing the frequencies so high that it would melt the human brain.

Leo activated it.

Leo screamed as his ears filled with pain. It was awful listening to such low and high-pitched screams.

The entire room vibrated around them but the Speaker kept talking. She wasn't affected.

Leo turned up the frequencies.

His ears hurt even more. Sebastian hugged him and Leo could tell he was in agony.

The Speaker wasn't reacting. She was laughing at them.

Leo deactivated the frequencies. And just stared at the Speaker as she watched them.

Sebastian started typing on the computer and Leo whipped out his gun, aimed at her and fired.

Of course the bullet melted in the shield but it made him feel good.

"I have it. I know exactly what frequency she operates at. And I know the exact counter-frequency. Thank you ex-boyfriend," Sebastian said.

Leo just grinned as the Speaker lost her smile and she actually looked terrified for a change.

"Do it," Leo said.

Sebastian flicked the switch and Leo loved feeling his body against his when Sebastian came over to him.

Half a second later the Speaker started screaming in pain as fake blood dripped out of her robot eyes and Leo was surprised that he didn't feel anything. Yet it was probably such a low frequency that it didn't affect humans.

The Speaker looked to be screaming out in agony as she fell to her knees and her hands clawed at the shields and looked to be begging for Leo to help her.

But there was no way in hell that he was ever going to help a person or robot like her because she was the traitor, the enemy and the tool that the Lord of War had tried to use to kill the Empire once and for all.

There was still her wave of data containing her speech being transmitted so Leo went over to the holographic computer, undocked her ship and ordered the Station to annihilate it.

Leo had to admit the explosion was very, very beautiful just not as beautiful and stunning as the handsome man standing next to him.

And that's when Leo realised Sebastian's shock collar was gone.

CHAPTER 20

Leo loved being back in the wonderful, delightful bridge of the *Emperor's Hammer* with the grey metal table showing the hologram of the rest of the Speaker's fleet retreating, the spherical walls showing how they were hunting down and picking the Speaker's fleet off one by one and Leo really, really loved the amazing company around him.

Marvin was busy swiping at the holograms and Quinn was studying the spherical walls intensely as she readjusted the firing solutions she was using.

Leo really did love them both because whilst him and Sebastian had been on the 99th Crimson Station, they had thankfully been working on containing as much as the Speaker's transmission as possible, and Quinn had even developed a counter transmission to send out and it appeared to have worked.

They were both so amazing and Leo really looked forward to working, laughing and being with them both until the day he died, because he actually liked the fact that no one left the Inquisition. You only died in the Inquisition.

Leo didn't mind that as the air stunk of wonderful peanut butter cookies, strong creamy coffee and little strawberry shortcakes that Quinn had baked earlier in preparation for Inquisitor Mason arriving himself.

Leo's stomach filled with butterflies at the idea of seeing his wonderful Master again, because Mason was just a great guy that was coming to congratulate them on stopping the threat whilst he had been busy dealing with other traitor threats, and he had come to past judgement on so-called criminal Sebastian.

As much as Leo wanted Mason to reveal all charges had been dropped, Leo didn't really want to get his hopes up because Mason could be a right hard ass when he wanted to be. And he didn't know Sebastian would like Mason very much either.

With Marvin and Quinn not looking at Leo, he took his hands off his guns hanging off his waist (something he hadn't actually realised he had been doing) and he subtly allowed his fingers to brush against beautiful Sebastian who was standing next to him.

Leo was surprised at how cool, smooth and relaxing Sebastian's touch was, and Leo never wanted this moment to end.

It was perfect in a way. It was perfect that it was the four of them that had worked so hard to defeat the traitors, they were all good friends (even Marvin had said well done to Sebastian through closed teeth) and they truly were unstoppable together.

"Inquisitor is aboard," Marvin said looking up and Leo didn't even dare take his fingers away from Sebastian's.

Quinn punched the air as the last of the traitor fleet was destroyed and she came over to them and Marvin joined, so they all stood at attention when Mason walked in and grinned at them all.

Leo smiled at Mason, a handsome tall middle-aged man wearing full black battle armour with a machine gun, cannon and sword hanging from his waist, and for some reason Mason looked extra happy today.

"My Lord," Marvin said bowing his head.

"At ease everyone, at ease," Mason said as they all gathered around the grey table. "I leave you all for two months and you get yourself in quite a little mess,"

Leo grinned.

"And somehow you all managed to pull yourself together, get the job done and help a criminal earn his freedom for a crime he never committed,"

The words slammed into Leo like a bear hug. He had no idea that Mason was going to admit it so easily that Sebastian wasn't a criminal.

"I have already entered the information on the Empire database and the liars have been arrested and sent to Penal colonies," Mason said.

Leo gulped, sending anyone to Penal Colonies

also known as dangerous mining worlds was an extreme punishment but clearly Mason liked Sebastian.

"Thank you my Lord," Sebastian said.

Mason waved him silent. "Don't be silly. Your shook collar fell off you without you interfering with it. That means that you are loyal solely to the Emperor and would happily die in His service,"

Leo hugged Sebastian and didn't care when he realised who he was in front of.

"So now I have to ask you a question," Mason said to Sebastian. "Do you want to go back to the Empire Army or join our little crew?"

Leo looked at Marvin in case he was going to protest but he frowned for a few moments before laughing.

"I would second that idea my Lord," Marvin said.

"Me too!" Quinn shouted by accident.

Sebastian laughed and smiled and looked completely shocked by the statements. "For the Emperor I accept. Only in death does duty end,"

"Only in death does duty end," everyone shouted in return before they all laughed a little and went back to their holograms and walls and finished off whatever their duties were.

Leo looked at the beautiful man that he had really fallen for over the past two months. And Leo realised that he had everything he had ever wanted, he had great friends, a job he loved that made a dramatic impact for the better on humanity and he finally, finally had a beautiful man that he could call his.

Life didn't exactly get much better than that.

SPEAKER OF TREACHERY

CHAPTER 21

A few hours later as he was laying in his brand-new quarters with a small orb of golden light floating about, Sebastian was utterly shocked and really pleased at what had happened today. He was finally a free man in the eyes of the Empire and everyone had finally realised just how much he loved the Emperor. Because at the end of the day, the Emperor represented everything that was good, pure and decent in the Empire.

Without him humanity really was like a species stumbling around the galaxy like the idiots some of them were.

Sebastian really loved the bright blue walls of his large quarters that came with a grey desk and chair, a holographic library filled with all the Empire knowledge and there was even a small kitchenette for him to enjoy. Sebastian had already been making a lot of use of the food synthesizer they had given him. It was even better that it also made different wonderful drinks.

The sound of the ship gently humming in the background was a good touch and Sebastian's little mug of his flat white hovered next to his bed just in case he wanted a small sip. And he was enjoying being here but he had to admit that it would be a lot better if stunning Leo was next to him with his strong bright red eyes staring into his.

Over the massive dinner Lord Mason had created for all of them, Sebastian had absolutely enjoyed every moment of it as they all laughed, joked and told breathtaking stories about all of their adventures. Sebastian was seriously looking forward to the future working with all of these wonderful people.

A moment later, Sebastian's door opened and Leo sneaked in and Sebastian didn't even need to be told to uncover some of the bed for Leo to climb into.

Sebastian watched wide-eyed as Leo climbed in naked next to him and Sebastian loved having such a beautiful man in his arms and having Leo snuggle into him.

"I did promise you a romantic talk," Leo said.

Sebastian laughed. "You were right about that and I like this talk so far, so we're actually doing this? Working together and being together. If so, I love that idea,"

Leo grinned like a little schoolboy. "Me too and yeah, we're doing this until we die,"

Sebastian of course didn't like the idea of one of

them dying but he was more than excited about spending the rest of his days with such a perfect man.

"Between you and me what did the Speaker show you when she, you know, influenced you?" Sebastian asked.

Leo weakly smiled and hugged him even more. "I just had this conversation with Mason and I think I'm lucky to still be alive, but the Speaker showed me an image of what happened when I was Empire Army,"

"You didn't tell me everything did you?" Sebastian asked.

Leo shook his head. "When I was running sabotage ops against the traitors I was doing them with the man I loved. We had been dating for so long that he was my rock, so one day we were hunting some traitor soldiers after we destroyed a power station they were using,"

Sebastian nodded.

"But Inquisitor Mason was already there on the planet hunting down the traitors as this was the moment the Empire finally broke through the defences. And Mason shot the man I loved. It was an accident but the man I loved died in my arms,"

Sebastian had no idea what to say to that.

"I fought Mason briefly. I actually bested him but he gave me a choice. I don't regret it at all. The choice was I could join him and get revenge on the traitors for making that situation possible or I could walk away and let my anger for the Inquisition kill me,"

Sebastian still didn't have anything to say.

Leo kissed him and Sebastian seriously hadn't expected his beautiful lips to be so smooth, warm and divine.

"I'm glad I choose to join him or I never would have met you. And you're far better than my ex anyway,"

"I'm glad too," Sebastian said kissing him back. "And Mason told me in private why she didn't affect me and why I survived the explosion,"

Leo sat up perfectly straight. "How?"

"It turns out when I first started in the Empire Army I served on a planet that was heavily radiated and we were never told about the radiation so we never wore protection. The conflict was over within two weeks so it wasn't long enough to kill us but I experienced mutations on the cellular level because of it,"

"And I'm guessing Mason took your DNA and cell samples like he did with us,"

Sebastian nodded. "He did and he discovered that my brain cells operate slightly differently to a normal human brain so that's why her corrupting frequency never worked on me. And the explosion was caused by her frequencies again not a real explosion. It caused the steel bars of the prison ship to vibrate so much they shattered and the prisoner's brains dissolved,"

Leo hugged him and kissed him hard. "I'm glad you're okay,"

Sebastian grinned at Leo. "You know we are

alone and are boyfriends now, want to make things interesting?"

Leo just laughed as Sebastian started kissing him, and Sebastian was really looking forward to finally exploring the beautiful, sexy, stunning man that he had fallen for and really wanted over the past two months.

And as they started to make love, the first time of many rounds that wonderful night, Sebastian just knew that they would get to know each other even better, fall in love with each other even more and make love more times than Sebastian ever thought possible.

Because he loved Leo far more than he ever thought it was possible to love another human and he knew that Leo felt the same way, and it was a truly wonderful, wonderful feeling.

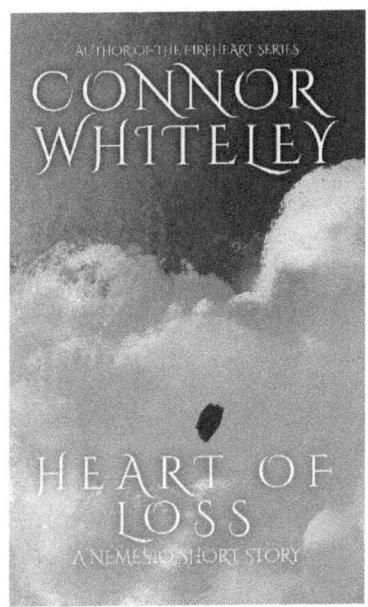

GET YOUR FREE AND EXCLUSIVE SHORT STORY NOW! LEARN ABOUT NEMESIO'S PAST!

https://www.subscribepage.com/fireheart

Keep up to date with exclusive deals on Connor Whiteley's Books, as well as the latest news about new releases and so much more!

Sign up for the Grab a Book and Chill Monthly newsletter, and you'll get one **FREE** ebook just for signing up: Agents of The Emperor Collection.

Sign Up Now!

https://dl.bookfunnel.com/f4p5xkprbk

About the author:

Connor Whiteley is the author of over 60 books in the sci-fi fantasy, nonfiction psychology and books for writer's genre and he is a Human Branding Speaker and Consultant.

He is a passionate warhammer 40,000 reader, psychology student and author.

Who narrates his own audiobooks and he hosts The Psychology World Podcast.

All whilst studying Psychology at the University of Kent, England.

Also, he was a former Explorer Scout where he gave a speech to the Maltese President in August 2018 and he attended Prince Charles' 70th Birthday Party at Buckingham Palace in May 2018.

Plus, he is a self-confessed coffee lover!

OTHER SHORT STORIES BY CONNOR WHITELEY

<u>Mystery Short Story Collections</u>

Criminally Good Stories Volume 1: 20 Detective Mystery Short Stories

Criminally Good Stories Volume 2: 20 Private Investigator Short Stories

Criminally Good Stories Volume 3: 20 Crime Fiction Short Stories

Criminally Good Stories Volume 4: 20 Science Fiction and Fantasy Mystery Short Stories

Criminally Good Stories Volume 5: 20 Romantic Suspense Short Stories

<u>Mystery Short Stories:</u>

Protecting The Woman She Hated

Finding A Royal Friend

Our Woman In Paris

Corrupt Driving

A Prime Assassination

Jubilee Thief

Jubilee, Terror, Celebrations

Negative Jubilation

Ghostly Jubilation

Killing For Womenkind

A Snowy Death

SPEAKER OF TREACHERY

Miracle Of Death
A Spy In Rome
The 12:30 To St Pancreas
A Country In Trouble
A Smokey Way To Go
A Spicy Way To GO
A Marketing Way To Go
A Missing Way To Go
A Showering Way To Go
Poison In The Candy Cane
Christmas Innocence
You Better Watch Out
Christmas Theft
Trouble In Christmas
Smell of The Lake
Problem In A Car
Theft, Past and Team
Embezzler In The Room
A Strange Way To Go
A Horrible Way To Go
Ann Awful Way To Go
An Old Way To Go
A Fishy Way To Go
A Pointy Way To Go
A High Way To Go
A Fiery Way To Go
A Glassy Way To Go

A Chocolatey Way To Go
Kendra Detective Mystery Collection Volume 1
Kendra Detective Mystery Collection Volume 2
Stealing A Chance At Freedom
Glassblowing and Death
Theft of Independence
Cookie Thief
Marble Thief
Book Thief
Art Thief
Mated At The Morgue
The Big Five Whoopee Moments
Stealing An Election
Mystery Short Story Collection Volume 1
Mystery Short Story Collection Volume 2
Criminal Performance
Candy Detectives
Key To Birth In The Past

<u>Science Fiction Short Stories:</u>
Temptation
Superhuman Autospy
Blood In The Redwater
All Is Dust
Vigil

Emperor Forgive Us
Their Brave New World
Gummy Bear Detective
The Candy Detective
What Candies Fear
The Blurred Image
Shattered Legions
The First Rememberer
Life of A Rememberer
System of Wonder
Lifesaver
Remarkable Way She Died
The Interrogation of Annabella Stormic
Blade of The Emperor
Arbiter's Truth
Computation of Battle
Old One's Wrath
Puppets and Masters
Ship of Plague
Interrogation
Edge of Failure
One Way Choice
Acceptable Losses
Balance of Power
Good Idea At The Time
Escape Plan
Escape In The Hesitation

Inspiration In Need
Singing Warriors
Knowledge is Power
Killer of Polluters
Climate of Death
The Family Mailing Affair
Defining Criminality
The Martian Affair
A Cheating Affair
The Little Café Affair
Mountain of Death
Prisoner's Fight
Claws of Death
Bitter Air
Honey Hunt
Blade On A Train
<u>Fantasy Short Stories:</u>
City of Snow
City of Light
City of Vengeance
Dragons, Goats and Kingdom
Smog The Pathetic Dragon
Don't Go In The Shed
The Tomato Saver
The Remarkable Way She Died
The Bloodied Rose
Asmodia's Wrath

Heart of A Killer
Emissary of Blood
Dragon Coins
Dragon Tea
Dragon Rider
Sacrifice of the Soul
Heart of The Flesheater
Heart of The Regent
Heart of The Standing
Feline of The Lost
Heart of The Story
City of Fire
Awaiting Death

Other books by Connor Whiteley:

Bettie English Private Eye Series
A Very Private Woman
The Russian Case
A Very Urgent Matter
A Case Most Personal
Trains, Scots and Private Eyes
The Federation Protects

Lord of War Origin Trilogy:
Not Scared Of The Dark
Madness
Burn Them All

The Fireheart Fantasy Series
Heart of Fire
Heart of Lies
Heart of Prophecy
Heart of Bones
Heart of Fate

City of Assassins (Urban Fantasy)
City of Death
City of Marytrs
City of Pleasure
City of Power

<u>Agents of The Emperor</u>
Return of The Ancient Ones
Vigilance
Angels of Fire
Kingmaker
The Eight
The Lost Generation
Hunt
Emperor's Council
Speaker of Treachery
Birth Of The Empire
Terraforma

<u>Lord Of War Trilogy (Agents of The Emperor)</u>
Not Scared Of The Dark
Madness
Burn It All Down

<u>The Garro Series- Fantasy/Sci-fi</u>
GARRO: GALAXY'S END
GARRO: RISE OF THE ORDER
GARRO: END TIMES
GARRO: SHORT STORIES
GARRO: COLLECTION
GARRO: HERESY
GARRO: FAITHLESS

GARRO: DESTROYER OF WORLDS
GARRO: COLLECTIONS BOOK 4-6
GARRO: MISTRESS OF BLOOD
GARRO: BEACON OF HOPE
GARRO: END OF DAYS

Winter Series- Fantasy Trilogy Books
WINTER'S COMING
WINTER'S HUNT
WINTER'S REVENGE
WINTER'S DISSENSION

Miscellaneous:
RETURN
FREEDOM
SALVATION
Reflection of Mount Flame
The Masked One
The Great Deer

Gay Romance Novellas
Breaking, Nursing, Repairing A Broken Heart
Jacob And Daniel
Fallen For A Lie
Spying And Weddings

All books in 'An Introductory Series':
Careers In Psychology
Psychology of Suicide
Dementia Psychology
Forensic Psychology of Terrorism And Hostage-Taking
Forensic Psychology of False Allegations
Year In Psychology
BIOLOGICAL PSYCHOLOGY 3RD EDITION
COGNITIVE PSYCHOLOGY THIRD EDITION
SOCIAL PSYCHOLOGY- 3RD EDITION
ABNORMAL PSYCHOLOGY 3RD EDITION
PSYCHOLOGY OF RELATIONSHIPS- 3RD EDITION
DEVELOPMENTAL PSYCHOLOGY 3RD EDITION
HEALTH PSYCHOLOGY
RESEARCH IN PSYCHOLOGY
A GUIDE TO MENTAL HEALTH AND TREATMENT AROUND THE WORLD- A GLOBAL LOOK AT DEPRESSION
FORENSIC PSYCHOLOGY
THE FORENSIC PSYCHOLOGY OF THEFT, BURGLARY AND OTHER

CRIMES AGAINST PROPERTY
CRIMINAL PROFILING: A FORENSIC PSYCHOLOGY GUIDE TO FBI PROFILING AND GEOGRAPHICAL AND STATISTICAL PROFILING.
CLINICAL PSYCHOLOGY FORMULATION IN PSYCHOTHERAPY
PERSONALITY PSYCHOLOGY AND INDIVIDUAL DIFFERENCES
CLINICAL PSYCHOLOGY REFLECTIONS VOLUME 1
CLINICAL PSYCHOLOGY REFLECTIONS VOLUME 2
Clinical Psychology Reflections Volume 3
CULT PSYCHOLOGY
Police Psychology

A Psychology Student's Guide To University
How Does University Work?
A Student's Guide To University And Learning
University Mental Health and Mindset

www.ingramcontent.com/pod-product-compliance
Lightning Source LLC
LaVergne TN
LVHW011840060526
838200LV00054B/4113